MW01487574

Murder
in
Little Heaven

Linda C. DeFew

ISBN-13: 978-1530915781

i

Illustrator

Not only is Alexa Black a gifted artist and a fellow writer, but she is also a neighbor and my friend. Her patience with me as I contemplated what scenes needed to be sketched to bring the story to life was greatly appreciated.

Contents

Prologue

The story of the 1927 murder on our property is something my husband, Eddie, and I have shared with many of our friends, but due to its length, we never have time to cover the whole thing. So, I have made it easy for you. The following is a condensed version based on a true story that will take you through the early days of Annie Laurie & Alvin Clemens to the death of Alvin and the trial of his wife, Annie Laurie. Some of the story comes from hearsay, but most is documented in the 740 pages of the transcript. Even though a few of the people involved are still alive today, they refuse to talk about the night of the murder. Some say they were threatened to the point of fearing for their lives and have proven that theory by a lifetime of secrecy.

The following story took place over 75 years ago. It is a matter of public knowledge and has been written strictly from a historical perspective. However, a few of the names have been changed to protect the privacy of local families. Our intention is to bring a cold case back to life, but make sure no one is offended in the process.

So, as you read the following pages, put yourself in the

jury seat and listen closely as each person is called to testify. Then, after all the evidence has been carefully weighed in your mind, make your own decision. Did the right person go to prison? Was there an accomplice? Who had the most to gain? Take your time and have fun. We'll be waiting for your verdict!

Chapter One
Spring 1995

Eddie and I came up to the old farmhouse one cool spring afternoon to see if the March flowers had come up yet. Sure enough, bright stalks of yellow blooms had found their way through the battered leaves of fall. I picked a bouquet between spring rain showers while Eddie popped a big bowl of popcorn. We were quite comfortable in our private country getaway. Our remodeling project of the 1920's house was slowly, but surely, bringing the old home place back to life. We were starting to think of it as our home away from home.

As we settled down by the old Warm Morning stove with a Coke and bowl of popcorn, we heard a soft knock at the door. Eddie got up and opened the door to find an elderly gentleman wearing a well-worn derby hat and a dark three-piece suit. A drop of rain dripped from the brim of his hat.

"Can I help you?" Eddie asked.

"I'm sorry to bother you, but I used to know the people who lived here," the gentleman said. "I was just wanting to see the old house. Would you mind?" he asked with a faint smile.

"Of course not. I'm Eddie Defew and my girlfriend, Linda, is in the living room. Come on in."

Eddie switched on the light in the foyer as the old man stepped inside. He couldn't keep from noticing the way the man was dressed. *His clothes are like my grandfather used to wear,* he thought. The old man stopped at the living room entrance, removed his hat, and looked inside.

"Come in and have a seat," Linda said.

"No, I can't," he replied staring blankly into the room. "I can only stay a minute." Suddenly, the old man's eyes filled with tears. She pretended not to notice.

"Did I understand you to say you knew Mrs. Katie?" Linda asked softly.

"No, ma'am, the young couple that lived here years ago." He took a handkerchief from his suit coat pocket and wiped his eyes. "This place sure brings back a lot of memories."

"Wait a minute," Eddie said. "Are you talking about the couple who lived here before Mrs. Katie?"

Derby Hat Left Behind

"Yes, a young couple with a small child. I was a young man then myself," he replied, pacing the hallway. "It was a horrible thing that happened here."

"So we've heard. We have so many questions we'd love to ask you," Eddie said, glancing anxiously at Linda. Some of the most significant questions surrounding the murder might be answered if we could only talk to him. After all, he knew the Clemens, didn't he?

The old gentleman removed his gold watch from his vest pocket and flipped open the cover. "Ah, it's getting late. I really should be going. My dinner's waiting."

"Give me a minute and I'll drive you home," Eddie said. "Just let me get my shoes."

"No, really, that won't be necessary. It's not that far." He turned to leave as Eddie held the front door for him.

"Come back anytime and, next time, please come and stay for a while."

Glancing back, he smiled sadly. "I'd love to. Goodbye for now."

Eddie closed the door and watched the old man walk away. A cold, eerie feeling engulfed him.

"Linda, is it just me or is it turning colder?"

"I don't think so. Hope you're not catching a cold."

Eddie turned up the heat a notch. The colored flames lit up the entire room.

"You know, Eddie, he never even told us his name," Linda commented.

"I know," he replied. "I wonder where he lives." He looked out again, but the visitor was nowhere in sight.

Eddie went to the foyer to turn off the light and there on

the library table layed the old man's hat.

"Linda, come on!" he yelled. "We've got to catch him. He left his hat."

We got in the truck and went down the road in the direction the old man had gone. The casual sprinkle was turning into a steady rain now. He didn't even have a raincoat. We had to find him before he got soaking wet. A man his age could get pneumonia in weather like this. We should have insisted he let us take him home, but it was too late now. We stopped by the nearest neighbor and asked if she had seen an old gentleman walking down the road.

"No, I haven't seen anybody. Weather's too bad for walking today."

We thanked her and turned back the other way. We scanned the roadside and the pastures. It was no use. The mysterious stranger had disappeared into thin air.

For weeks to come, we asked everyone around if they had seen this old man. We described him to everyone in the neighborhood. He was an average size man of medium build. From what he had said, he would have to be in his 90's, but the years had been very kind to him. He appeared strong and healthy. His clothes looked new as if he had just stepped out of an 1890's Sears and Roebuck catalog. Unfortunately, no one had seen him or even heard of such a man. We finally gave up and decided it was just one of those things that can never be explained.

Then, on January 15, 1996, one year into our renovation, the old house burned to the ground. All our hard work was destroyed in a matter of minutes. The insurance arson investigator wrote it up as faulty wiring, but the exact cause was never determined. It was a big disappointment, but after spending so much time at the farm, we both had grown to love it and decided to make it our home. We built a new house, married that fall, and started a new life together.

During the coming months, we met many people from the community. Several neighbors offered their stories that had been handed down through the years. We heard the same line over and over. "You do know there was a murder committed here, don't you?" Sure, we had heard it. The story came with the property, but no two stories were alike. Every time we heard a new version, the more curious we became. One day, we decided enough was enough. It was time to get serious and find out the truth.

First, we called the courthouse and were told the trial transcript was missing. The clerk said the folder was there,

Clemens vs. State of Kentucky, but the contents were gone. No one knew why. For days, they searched the courthouse. It was useless. The entire record of the trial was gone. It took some time, but we didn't give up. Before long, we obtained a copy of the murder trial transcript that had been missing for years.

We couldn't wait! Page by page, the whole thing unfolded right before our eyes. Nothing was as we had been told. We now saw the murder in a whole new light; one shaded in secrets and lies.

Linda C. DeFew

Chapter Two
Annie & Alvin's Life Together

Annie Laurie Fitzgerald & Marion Alvin Clemens met in 1915, in Marion, Illinois, at the Calumet Baking Powder Company where they both were employed. Annie was a demonstrator of the baking product and Alvin was a traveling salesman. But, that was the only thing they had in common. Annie was a pretty well-to-do city girl from Quitman, Georgia, the exact opposite of Alvin, a down-home country boy from Slocum, Kentucky, just trying to get by.

Newlyweds

All the single girls in the small community mourned the day Alvin left town. Although shy with the ladies, he was definitely the most handsome man in Slocum -- tall and lean, a perfect gentleman. But, it was impossible to turn Alvin's head no matter how hard they tried.

That all changed with Annie. Alvin thought she was quite possibly the most beautiful girl he had ever seen. When her dark brown eyes met his, he thought he had died and gone to heaven. Her long, dark hair fell down her back like sheets of silk just begging to be touched. As far as Alvin was concerned, Annie was perfect. He had to make her his own, so on March 15, 1917, after a brief courtship, Annie & Alvin were married. Annie was a mere child of 17 while Alvin was a grown man, 28 years old.

Annie quit her job and went on the road with Alvin for the next two years. In the fall of 1919, they learned they were going to have a child. They were excited with the idea of becoming parents, but some changes would have to be made. They decided that Annie would move in with her father that next spring and stay until the baby was born. Marion Alvin Clemens, Jr., arrived in the world on May 24, 1920. Now they were truly a family. Alvin felt a grave responsibility to settle down and make a home for his son. As soon as Annie and the baby were able to travel, Alvin brought his southern bell wife and baby boy to his farm in Kentucky. He had dreamed of this day for years and had never been happier, but it wasn't exactly what Annie had expected.

The Bradshaw's owned a cabin next to the Clemens' farm and had offered to let them use it until they could get their own house built. Her heart sank when she saw the little one-room house waiting for their arrival. She had envisioned a snug little cabin nestled in the woods, a romantic hideaway like in the movies. But this wasn't Hollywood. Annie had never seen such a wilderness and the Bradshaw place was hardly more than a shack. Alvin assured her it was only temporary, and she made the best of it. Besides, they were so much in love, nothing else mattered.

New Home For Annie

On December 9, 1922, Alvin held good to his promise

and, with the help of some good neighbors, the family of three moved into their new bungalow-style house. The place was a mansion compared to the little house they had occupied for the past two years. The first floor consisted of a kitchen and a parlor -- a fireplace in each room -- divided by a foyer that went from the front door to the back. A full attic served as a bedroom with dormer windows in the front. A long front porch stretched the length of the house facing Slocum Road. Annie loved her new house and did all she could to make it a home.

Although raised in the south, Annie adjusted pretty well to country life in the Ohio Valley region. Summers were much the same as Georgia, but the winters were quite different. Colder temperatures with ice and snow were in vast contrast to the mild winters down south. Back home, she could walk uptown for groceries or enjoy an afternoon matinee any season of the year. But this was different. The nearest town was miles away and getting out of Slocum in the fall and winter was almost impossible. The temperatures were cold enough at night to freeze the muddy roads to sheets of ice, and the days weren't much better. The temperatures warmed up slightly above freezing, thawing the surface to a slick wet muck. Mule teams became the only means of travel. Often, one of the local farmers would drive them to Carrsville once a week to pick up supplies for the entire community.

Annie took pride in being self-sufficient. Other than the basic staples – coffee, corn meal, sugar, and flour -- she rarely needed anything else. Her chickens and turkeys supplied the family with eggs and meat and a good Jersey cow produced all the milk they needed. Along with the vegetables she canned from her garden, Annie made sure they never went hungry.

Still, times were tough. Alvin wanted more for his wife and child than to just get by. Farming income wasn't enough, so in 1923, when Junior was three, he took a job on the road with the *Jell-O* Company. The arrangement was perfect for him. He could farm in the spring and summer, then, supplement that income as a salesman through the fall and winter.

For Alvin, it was an answer to his prayers. Bright and ambitious, he came on board just as *Jell-O* became a favorite wintertime treat. Since its invention in 1897, the fruit-flavored dessert had steadily grown in popularity, and by 1925, the company was well on their way to becoming one of the most successful companies in the United States.

The Internet provides us with a brief insight into the company's early days: "*Jell-O's* history boasts of training their well-groomed, well-versed in the art of selling employees to use advertising and merchandising methods never before employed. They were sent out in spanking rigs drawn by beautiful horses into the roads, byroads, fairs, country gatherings, church socials, and parties to advertise their product. First came team-drawn wagons, to be followed by smart auto-cars. Pictures, posters, and billboards over the American landscape, as well as page ads in magazines, carried the *Jell-O* Girl and the six delicious flavors into the American home." Alvin fit their marketing plan to a tee.

As Alvin was preparing to leave that fall, Annie's parents invited her and Junior to come and spend the winter with them in Florida. She jumped at the chance. Lately, she had become restless and discontent. A change might be just what she needed. But a few days before they left, a nearby neighbor, Ray Baker, paid her an unexpected visit. He had become enthralled with her the day he met her, and he simply couldn't let her go without telling her how crazy he was about her.

From Florida, she wrote him a letter that ignited a two-year relationship. She loved the attention of an older man, and she had no problem wrapping him around her little finger. Ray was a single man in his forties who had never been in love and fell head over heels for Annie.

When Annie and Alvin returned to their home in the spring of 1924 , Annie saw Ray nearly every day. Of course, they had to be secretive. They planned their rendezvous at times and places no one would suspect. But, despite her careful planning, rumors of her indiscretions spread like hot butter throughout the community. From the beginning, most of the people had suspected she was not what she seemed. She had an eye for the men and made no attempt to hide it. However, if her reputation had been in question before, now it was ruined. But, because they hated to see Alvin hurt, nobody said a word to him. He would know soon enough.

Another summer came and went with a drought that made the season a challenge even for the strongest man. Working from daylight to dark, Alvin hardly had the time or energy to spend analyzing his wife. If he noticed a change in her, he felt it best to let it go. Things would be better in time. Before they knew it, the leaves were changing colors, and it was time to leave again.

That winter, Annie spent her time in Florida working at a real estate office. She began to make money like she had never thought possible. The '20's were a boom time for the sunshine state. People were moving there from all over the country and property was selling at a phenomenal rate.

Alvin's letters to her during that second winter bear out the fact that she had second thoughts about even coming back to Kentucky at all. He was devastated and pleaded with her to reconsider. Alvin would do anything to save his marriage and keep his son. He promised her he would take a shorter route next winter that would take only six weeks to complete. After that, he would submit his resignation. But he also went a step further. He said they would move away from Slocum after taking care of matters at home. It broke his heart, but he wanted Annie to be happy. Knowing he was a man of his word, Annie and Junior came home on the next train.

On January 1, 1927, Alvin left for his final assignment with *Jell-O*. Annie and Junior stayed home, but not without help. Before Alvin left, he hired a 15-year-old neighbor girl, Ruby, to stay with Annie and Junior. When he sent his paycheck to Annie each week, he also sent Ruby the four dollars a week they had agreed upon. Ruby was happy with her job and caught on fast. She was young, but wiser than most girls her age. She was good with Junior and, before long, she was doing most of the cooking and milking. Now, with more time to concentrate on her poultry and cows, Annie sold eggs to the local grocery and sweet cream to the dairy.

In spite of her disputable character, one couldn't help but admire Annie Laurie in some ways. She was independent and strong-willed, able to do a day's work the same as any man. Help was always available. Out of respect for Alvin, the neighborhood men pitched in if her fences needed mending or her woodpile got low while her husband was away. He would do the same for them. Annie was grateful and went out of her way to show it. She had a way of charming the men, but the women saw right through her.

Alvin hadn't been gone two weeks before another rumor spread through the small community. Annie was involved with another man and, this time, he was seven years younger and married. Now, the women really shunned her, but that didn't bother her anymore. She turned to men for friendship, and there was always one willing to be her friend.

In time, they taught her to shoot and hunt like one of the boys. Ruby watched Junior for a few hours a day while Annie went hunting for their supper. She loved the outdoors, but more than that, she loved the attention she received from all her new male friends. She found herself dreading the day

Alvin would come back home. Maybe it was because her thoughts were not with her husband anymore. She would have to be careful. He couldn't know how much her feelings had changed. If he found out, she could lose the most important thing in the world to her -- Junior. Whatever it took, Alvin couldn't find out the truth.

Chapter Three
Alvin's Return

By the end of January, Alvin was home with his family for good. By then, Ruby had become such a valued part of their family, her parents gave her permission to stay and work for the Clemens. It worked out well for both parties — she put in a good day's work for them, and, at the same time, made herself a little money.

As time went on, Alvin noticed his good friend, Ray, was avoiding him. Alvin questioned Annie, so she had no choice but to come clean about their relationship before he found out on his own. She told him everything, even let him read Ray's love letters. Of course, Ray was not the only man in her life, but Alvin didn't know that. He believed his wife had made one mistake, and she wanted to put it behind her. So, in an effort to restore his marriage, he confessed to her that she had not done any worse that he had. He said he had visited the "red light" district while in Philadelphia and had regretted it ever since. Afterward, they both vowed to "live together and be true to one another" for their son's sake.

Meanwhile, the people in Slocum welcomed Alvin back

home. On March 16, 1927, a dance was planned in his honor down the road at Harrison Adams' house. All the community was invited. Annie told Ruby to call her friend, Sylvia, who was staying with Ray's sick mother, to see if she could go to the dance with them and spend the night afterward. Sylvia said Mrs. Baker needed her and refused to let her go home with Ruby.

Later, Sylvia, Annie, Junior, and Ruby paid a visit to her the afternoon of the dance, but this time, Sylvia said her parents had also told her she couldn't go. Several neighbors were at the house and gathered in the sitting room to listen to the radio and talk. During the visit, Annie and Ray left the room and were gone for about thirty minutes. When they came back, Annie insisted that Sylvia come home with them and, despite what her parents or Mrs. Baker had said, she didn't argue. Along with Ruby, Sylvia would spend the night at the Clemens' house, too.

Just after dark, Alvin, Annie, Junior, Ruby, Sylvia, and Roy Singleton, a close neighbor, walked from the Clemens' down to the Adams' house. A bright glow from the huge bonfire lit up the entire sky. The whole community had turned out -- that is, except for Ray.

Horses and wagons lined the lane leading to the barn.

Music filled the air. Everyone that played an instrument had brought it along and was joining in the fun. All the ladies brought their favorite dishes, and the children roasted hot dogs. Alcohol was abundant and, as the night wore on, it started to show.

Annie danced every dance, loving every minute of it, but a slow dance between her and Orville Adams ended the celebration for the Clemens. Alvin didn't like it. The way he saw it, they were standing too close and looking too deep into each other's eyes. Anyone could see a fight was brewing between the two men. Several people overheard Orville trying to borrow a pistol to show Alvin a thing or two. But Annie knew how to handle her husband. She turned on her charm and calmed him down with a little sweet-talking. Reluctantly, Alvin picked up Junior and he and Annie left along with the two teenage girls and their boyfriends.

It was midnight by the time they got to the Clemens' home, so Annie, Alvin, and Junior undressed by the fireplace in the parlor then went to bed upstairs. The attic was equipped with two beds that could be used when they had guests. Annie had given Ruby and Sylvia permission to stay outside and talk to the boys a few minutes before they went to bed. When the boys left, the teenage girls retired to the featherbed in the parlor. But the night was not over. Within two short hours, each one of their lives would be changed forever.

Chapter Four
March 17, 1927
(The Night of the Murder)

This chapter is my rendition of the night Alvin was killed. It is based on facts, but with a bit of my own creation as to how the characters would most likely have interacted under those circumstances.

The staircase creaked with every step as the young girl hurried up the narrow passage to the cold, dark attic. Aware of the child sleeping in the next bed, she spoke just above a whisper, but the urgency was clear.

"Annie! Annie! Wake up!" Ruby said, nudging Annie Laurie's shoulder.

Annie shielded her eyes from the bright glow of the coal oil lamp. "Okay, Ruby, I'm awake," she replied with growing aggravation. "Put down that lamp. What in the world's wrong with you?"

"It's Alvin," Ruby answered. "He woke me up, told me to come up here and sleep with you. Annie, he was acting real strange." The girl looked down, too embarrassed to tell what Alvin had really said.

Annie tried to clear the sleep from her head. "Oh, Ruby, you're dreaming. Alvin is right here," she mumbled, feeling the covers next to her. She threw the brightly colored quilts back with one toss when she realized his side was empty. She jumped up, getting angrier by the minute. "Alvin, you know how much I hate being woke up in the middle of the night!" she huffed. "Just wait till I get my hands on you!"

The young girl stood by Annie's bed, rubbing her skinny arms briskly. Her teeth had begun to chatter, and huge tears streaked down her cheeks. "Hurry, Annie," she sobbed. "I'm scared."

"Here! Get in this bed before you catch cold!" She held the covers while Ruby crawled into the bed's soft, warm covers. The March night was unseasonably cold, and the only heat in the bedroom drifted up the stairwell from the fireplace on the first floor.

"I'll take care of Alvin, but no sense in both of us freezing to death in the meantime." She wouldn't take it out on Ruby. It was obvious this was no childhood nightmare.

"I don't know what's got into that man, but I'm going to get to the bottom of it right now!" she said as she covered her cotton nightgown with a long flannel robe that hung by

26

the attic door. "I'll be right back, Ruby. This won't take long." She picked up the lamp and stormed down the creaking staircase.

It had all started at the dance that night down at the Adams' house. Just a few hours ago, she had been having a wonderful time dancing with a handsome twenty-year-old man. For some unknown reason, Alvin had gotten jealous. Words were exchanged, and Annie had stepped between them to prevent a fight. It had been a stressful situation. Now this!

When she reached the foyer, Annie glanced at the old grandfather clock at the end of the hall. Two o'clock. Its loud chimes struck just as she peeped into the parlor. The next thing she knew, a shotgun blast lit up the house like a flash of lightning. Frozen in panic, Annie stood staring at her husband's lifeless body. She heard Sylvia screaming, but couldn't move or say a word. Ruby came bounding down the stairs and stopped short when she saw Annie's pale face.

"Annie! What's wrong?" she cried.

"I don't know! I don't know! I heard a scream and then he was on the floor." She put her hand over her mouth, her whole body beginning to shake.

Girls with Annie Following Shooting

You can't lose it now, Annie. Pull yourself together. She closed her eyes and took a deep breath. "Sylvia, call your father and tell him to come over right now! Ruby, go see about Junior!" Both girls obeyed without a word.

Ruby ran back up the stairs expecting to find Junior awake and scared. To her surprise, the cotton-top seven-year-old was still sleeping. Thank goodness he was a sound sleeper.

"Ruby! Is he still asleep?" Annie yelled from down below.

"Yeah, I don't know how, but he is," she answered, hurrying back down the stairs.

"Okay . . . good." She took their hands in hers. "Sylvia, Ruby, you've got to go with me to get help."

"But . . ." Sylvia stuttered.

"Hush . . .don't talk! Just listen to me," she demanded as she told them her plan. Then, tightening her grip, she said, "We have to go get help for Alvin."

Ruby didn't question. She'd known Annie for a long time, and she didn't want to cross her now. Her eyes looked strange, like a wild animal looking for an escape. Annie hooked a girl on each arm, and the three of them stepped out into the cold night. The moon made it easy to find their way down to the road.

It was quiet for the moment, but Annie knew that within minutes everyone would know what had happened. A call going out in the middle of the night would send an alarm throughout the entire community. They were all on the same party line and listening in on a neighbor's call was common. It was just a matter of time.

Annie Confronted by Neighbors

Suddenly, they heard voices coming closer and closer. Annie screamed for help, and a couple of local boys, Turk Trail, and Herman Ferrell came running toward the girls.

"What happened, Mrs. Clemens? they asked, bending over to catch their breath.

Annie was explaining what had happened when Ora Suits and Odell Adams arrived. From out of the dark, Orville, Odell's brother, jumped the fence to join them. He and Ora offered to go with her back to the house. Someone had to check to see if Alvin was dead. When they got back, Ora made the announcement: "He's as dead as he'll ever be."

The news shocked the small community of Slocum. Before long, people began arriving on foot and on horseback from both directions at the same time. They formed a circle around her, staring in disbelief. She stared back into cold, judgmental eyes. What had she expected? They had never accepted her. Why would this be any different?

"What's wrong with you people?" Annie shouted hysterically, wiping the tears that now fell freely down her cheeks. "Why don't somebody call the sheriff?"

"He's already been called, Annie," Sylvia's father answered as he folded his arms across his chest and looked down at the ground.

"Oh, that's . . . uh . . . good . . . I guess," Annie stammered, rubbing her cold hands together. The ramification of the crime had started to hit home. These people had looked for seven years to find some way to get rid of her. This was their chance. Obviously, she had wasted her time trying to win their friendship. Her only hope was Dr. Masoncup. He was a good man. He would understand. He had too.

The doctor arrived in his usual style, sitting tall on his big black stallion, wearing a black trench coat and carrying a worn out leather bag. He looked down at Annie. "Is he dead, Annie?" he asked in a deep, calm voice.

"Yes, he's dead, Doc. What am I going to do?" she

pleaded.

"Get on," he demanded.

She took Doc's strong hand and rode straddle behind him, a practice the other women snubbed from the day she arrived in Slocum. Refusing to ride a horse side-saddle was proof enough to them that this woman was no lady. The rest of the group followed behind them either on foot or horse-back.

Once inside the house, Doc asked the others to wait in the kitchen while he and Annie went into the parlor. They stared in silence at the lifeless body lying face down on the plank floor. A narrow stream of bright red blood flowed from his chest filling the room with a putrid sweet odor. Doc knelt down and felt for a pulse. He shook his head and gently put a towel under his head where blood ran from his mouth. The humility of that simple action sent shock waves through Annie. Doc loved this man. They all did. *They're going to kill me!* she thought.

Fear and exhaustion suddenly replaced the adrenaline that had been rushing through her for almost an hour. Feeling the bile rising from her stomach, she ran to the back door sick from nerves and panic that now wracked her body.

Weak and numb, she welcomed Ruby's offer to help. She leaned against her knowing she would collapse without support. Then she remembered her son.

"I've got to go check on Junior. I can't let him see this," Annie said, pulling away from Ruby.

"He's okay, Annie," Ruby assured her. "Mrs. Adams carried him over to her house. She'll take good care of him."

"Oh, dear, what will happen to my little boy?" she cried.

"Don't you go worrying about that right now, ya hear? Just rest for a while," Ruby said as she led her toward the kitchen.

Why is everybody whispering? Annie thought as she passed through the mirage of people.

Without warning, the floor started rising up to meet her, and everything went black. The next thing she knew, she was sitting on a soft pallet by the fireplace in the kitchen and someone was holding a tin cup to her mouth urging her to sip from its warm contents. She recognized the smell of lemon and honey mixed with a generous portion of Al's best whiskey. Grateful for the alcohol's soothing effect, she curled herself into a tight ball, wishing she could just disappear. Muffled voices in the distance echoed in her ears.

"I don't believe it. Not Annie."

"She must be mad."

"Poor Alvin."

"I've never trusted her."

She covered her ears with her hands trying to make the voices stop. Even then, the blast of the shotgun still reverberated in her ears. It had all happened so fast. A slight buzz from the hot liquid began to cloud her thoughts. She couldn't let it. She had to think straight. The sheriff had been sent for and would return with the coroner's jury. Questions would have to be answered, and it was imperative that she remained focused. Suddenly, it became hard to distinguish what was truth and what was made up. That was something she had to keep straight. Annie hoped she had made Ruby and Sylvia understand how important it was that they all tell the same story.

"This is the way it happened," she had stressed to the girls as they left the house just minutes after the incident. "Don't ever change the story I told you, or you'll be sorry!"

Never in her life had she ever threatened a living soul. She hated herself for doing it now, but it was the only way. When the people heard her story, they would have to believe it regardless of how they felt about her. Of course, she had her faults. She'd be the first to admit that. But didn't they all? Needless to say, tonight wouldn't be easy to explain. A crime of passion never was. But, if she could make them believe it, they would let her go. Then she'd get to keep her son and put this horrible night behind her.

"You have to believe me! You have to! Please!" she cried from somewhere deep inside her nightmarish state.

"Annie, wake up! You're dreaming!" Ruby yelled, holding her tightly. "It's almost noon, Annie. You have to wake up now."

Annie opened her eyes and grabbed Ruby's arm. "Tell me it was a dream, Ruby!" She knew better. Standing behind Ruby was Deputy Sheriff Bryant. He knelt down beside her.

"Annie, the coroner's inquest is about to conclude. We are ready to take your statement now." His voice was kind but stern.

Walking in a daze, Annie took his hand and followed

him into the room where Alvin lay. Quiet and somber, a group of six men sat around the room staring at the body. Not one of them would look her in the eyes.

Annie Taken to Jail

"I guess you can see what I have done," Annie said through trembling lips.

"Does that mean you're prepared to sign a confession?" the coroner asked.

"Yes. I will sign it," Annie said, taking the pen from his hand. A sigh of relief filled the room when she signed her name on the form. They had spent all afternoon in the company of death, and the stress was starting to show.

"Ok, gentlemen, this concludes the coroner's inquest.

You will be notified of the court date, but for now, you are free to go."

The men filed past Annie as if she wasn't there. In tears, each one stopped at Alvin's feet to silently pay their respects to a dear friend. Coroner Boyd followed them to the door to thank them for their help and to answer any questions.

Left alone, Annie sat staring out the window to avoid looking at Alvin. She was getting sicker by the minute. *I can't stay here in this room.* She leaned her forehead against the cool windowpane to stop her head from spinning.

After seeing the jury out, the coroner walked to her side. "Annie, Deputy Bryant will take you in now."

"But . . ." Annie pleaded.

"No, no, not now. We'll have plenty of time to talk later," the deputy replied, reaching for her hand. She hesitated for a few seconds but then complied. There was nothing more to discuss.

He helped her into her coat while Ruby went to get her shoes. She felt a strong arm firmly guiding her down the hall and out the back door.

The people filed out one by one behind her. Annie stared

back at the accusing faces of her neighbors as she was put in the sheriff's car. There would be a trial, a jury would be selected, and, eventually, she would get to tell her story. But Annie had learned two important things living among these people. First and foremost, country folks stick together through thick and thin; and second, blood truly is thicker than water. Alvin was one of their own. Would anything he had done really matter to them? How could she convince them that he was the one at fault?

Chapter Five
Coroner's Inquest

F. M. Boyd, the local hardware merchant, arrived at the Clemens' home around ten o'clock on the morning following the murder. He also held the positions of undertaker and county coroner. He had called his jury early that morning, and they were waiting at the Clemens' house when he arrived.

The sheriff led them through the crowd to the parlor where Alvin Clemens, 38, lay full-length, face-down just inside the doorway. The men sat silently in a circle and watched as the coroner examined the lifeless body. A small stream of blood led to a pool near his chest, but no wounds were evident. The coroner carefully turned the body over. Alvin's blood-saturated left hand rigidly covered a gaping hole in his left breast. Coagulated blood gathered thickly around the wound. There was no doubt what had caused his death.

The shotgun, propped behind the front door, was brought out and examined along with the two wads lying on the parlor floor. The coroner scribbled in his tablet: Victim shot in chest with 12-gauge, breech-loading, double-barrel shotgun at a distance of six to eight feet, resulting in immediate death.

Their attention was then directed toward Alvin's clothing and its condition. Every button on his cream colored, lightweight union suit was buttoned. The impact had left a jagged tear and the area around it was soaked in blood.

Next, each member of the coroner's jury was asked to make an inspection of the 14' x 14' room where the murder occurred. They questioned the absence of blood. It did not take an expert to see that there was not enough blood for the man to have been shot at close range. One man said there was no more blood on the floor than could have fit in both his hands cupped together. Several splatters were present on the threshold and wall, but still not enough to justify such an explosion.

The furniture was examined for anything that looked out of the ordinary. The room was not unlike many parlors of the day -- a small chair, a nightstand, a sewing machine, a piano, a trunk, and a three-quarter-size feather bed. Its soft billows held impressions of the persons who had slept there the night before. The outside showed the imprint of a large adult stretching the entire length of the bed, but the one on the inside was definitely a small person, probably a child no more than three foot tall. It was noted that of the two girls that supposedly slept there, Ruby was a small woman of 102 pounds, while Sylvia was much larger. Junior, the only child in the house that night, was said to have been upstairs with his parents.

Contents of Pocket

Several articles of Alvin's clothing were present in the parlor -- shoes, socks, overalls, and a sweater -- the ones he had removed before going upstairs the night before. On the nightstand, a pair of brass knuckles, a watch, and a closed pocketknife served as grim reminders of the man who would no longer need them.

Finally, a meticulous survey of the rest of the house was done, both inside and out. Only one thing appeared out of the ordinary. A screen on the north window of the parlor had been torn in one corner and pulled downward. The shade on that window was also raised slightly while the ones on the east side were lowered all the way. They found nothing else unusual, so they gathered back inside for the conclusion.

Mr. Boyd motioned to the deputy, and he escorted Annie to the parlor. "I guess you can see what I've done," she said with a stone face. She saw no need to explain. They had seen the evidence for themselves.

The jury looked away from her in disgust. It was written on each solemn face. She had killed their neighbor and friend. They wanted justice even if they had to take the matter into their own hands. Tension was high. A wrong look or a harsh word could send contained emotions out of control. Just in time, the undertaker's buckboard pulled up for the corpse. Each jury member helped the driver place Alvin's body on a slab and carried it out to the wagon.

Annie watched them leave, each one a close friend of her dead husband. She should have known. They had never accepted her and, now that Alvin was gone, they treated her like a complete stranger. If this jury was any example of what she would face in court, she would be going away for a very long time.

Linda C. DeFew

Chapter Six
Contents of Trunk

At 3:45 a.m. on March 17th, Lucian Clemens, the dead man's brother, woke up out of a deep sleep to the sound of a pounding fist on his back door. No doubt something bad had happened. News coming at that time of night was never good.

"Come quick! Alvin's been shot!" Ollie Kimsey shouted when Lucian opened the door.

He waited while Lucian rushed to get dressed; then, they rode together as fast as their mules would take them to his brother's house. Fear and confusion filled his head. Surely it was an accident. Why would anyone want to hurt Alvin?

Two miles was all that separated his house from his brother's, but it might as well have been ten. It was the longest ride of his life. When he arrived and saw Alvin laying on the parlor floor, he realized all the hurrying in the world wouldn't have helped him. There was nothing anybody could do. Although his body was still warm, Alvin was dead.

Lucian went straight to the kitchen where Annie was

and demanded an explanation. She recounted her story to him from start to finish, trying to convince her brother-in-law that it was all Alvin's fault. He held his temper and let her finish.

"I just couldn't take any more," she said tearfully.

"Don't you know you took the worst way out? Didn't you think about the boy?" Lucian yelled.

"I guess I should have thought about that," she said humbly.

Listening to her sobs just made matters worse. Lucian felt a fierce rage taking the place of shock. He didn't know what to believe at this point, but the story he had just been told didn't sound like something his brother would do. He knew him too well. He told the sheriff he was leaving for a few hours. He had to get some fresh air. As he was leaving, Annie offered her hand to him, but he waved her off and said, "I have nothing to say to you." His brother was dead at the hand of this woman. He wasn't buying her "I loved him so much I killed him" attitude. Something told him there was a lot she wasn't telling. She had done nothing but bring disgrace to his family name ever since she had moved here and now this.

Alvin's Grave Scene

A few hours later, Lucian came back to find the house filled to capacity with well-meaning friends and relatives. Out of respect for his brother, he greeted each one and thanked them for their thoughtfulness, but he was there for another reason. Deputy Bryant had asked Lucian earlier if he would take possession of the house and property while Annie was incarcerated. He gladly accepted. It was his brother's house, and he would see that everything was taken care of.

As Annie was leaving for jail, she stopped in front of Lucian and reluctantly handed him the house key. He was relieved to see her go. It had been a long day. When everyone had gone, he quickly locked up the house and went to take care of the funeral arrangements.

The next day, Alvin's funeral was held at the Presbyterian Church in the town of Carrsville, just a few miles from where his life had ended. He was buried on a high hill in the town cemetery overlooking the Ohio River. From the size of the crowd, Alvin would be remembered for years to come.

Three days later, Lucian called his friends, Harry Crawford and Hugh Bennett and asked them to go with him back to his brother's house. He wanted to do a little investigating on his own but wanted to make sure he had witnesses. The men were glad to help.

First and foremost in Lucian's mind was to examine the contents of Annie's steamer trunk. Over the years, he had heard Annie speak of it when referring to keepsakes or personal papers. If she was keeping anything secret, chances are he would find answers inside.

But, just as he had expected, it was locked tight. That didn't matter to him. He would break the lock if he had too. He got down and looked closer. The lock was simple. Maybe, just maybe . . . He dug in his pocket and, as luck would have it, the key to the trunk of his Roadster worked like a charm. He opened it cautiously unsure of what he would find. Nothing in the tray on top looked unusual, just the normal things you would expect to find in a trunk -- some of Junior's baby clothes and a couple of Annie's dresses. He removed the tray carefully. Underneath, he found piles of newspapers, books, and bundles of letters neatly tied together with twine. He lifted one large stack to find a picture of Raymond Baker staring back at him.

Lucein Looking in Trunk

Lucian sat down hard on the wooden floor beside the trunk. It hit him like a kick in the gut. Why was he surprised? He had heard the talk the same as everyone else, but he had always hoped that they were just rumors. Thinking back, he had seen Annie and Ray together a lot, especially when Alvin was gone. Now, thumbing through the letters, his worst suspicions were confirmed. It didn't take long to see that the majority of them were from the man in the picture, only a few from his brother.

Lucian was anxious to read the letters but knew this wasn't the place to do it. He would trust his two friends with his life, but if the wrong person came by and found him tampering with evidence, he would be in deep trouble. He loaded the letters in a sack and locked the trunk. This time, he nailed the front and back doors of the house shut. With each swing of the hammer, he made a promise, "Alvin, my brother; justice will be done. I won't let her get away with any more lies."

Lucian spent days mulling over the letters. Each one made his blood boil just to think that right under Alvin's nose, his so-called "friend" was having an affair with his wife. To make matters worse, Ray and Alvin were more than friends. They had grown up together in the little community of Slocum just a couple of miles apart. They hunted and fished together and were always there for each other when one of them needed help on the farm. Ray was one of the first to greet them when Alvin brought Annie back to his Kentucky home. Annie instantly liked him and loved to listen to the stories he and Alvin shared of their childhood days.

Without a doubt, Ray led a very interesting life. He was an adventurer and outdoorsman, somewhat of a local hero.

Men and women alike enjoyed his company. He had big plans for the future, but, for now, he had to stay home to help his father run the family farm. When Ray's mother got sick, he promised his father he would be there as long as they needed him. Ray was a man of his word.

On the other hand, Alvin was just a poor, hard-working man. He had tried so hard to make Annie happy, working night and day to give her the things she wanted and needed. If only Lucian had told him about the rumors during their last conversation, Alvin might have seen it coming. Now it was too late.

A few weeks before the trial, Lucian returned to his brother's house once more to make sure he hadn't over-looked anything. Something kept bugging him. The days following the killing, he had devoted his attention to the rooms downstairs, but he had completely ignored the room upstairs. This time he went up there first. There was little to see -- two beds, one full and one twin, a couple of jackets hanging on nails and, over in a dark corner, a wardrobe trunk! It didn't even have a lock. Why hadn't he noticed it before?

Using a lantern to brighten the room, he quickly threw open the lid. To his surprise, bloody rags held down by the heavy weight sprang up at him. *So this is what you used to wipe up the blood, Annie old girl! No wonder there was so little at the scene.* But why would she do that?

Lucian didn't have the answers, but he felt justice was just around the corner. He was glad he had come back. Now he was certain that this evidence, along with the letters, would seal her fate forever. He couldn't wait to tell it all in court. As far as Lucian was concerned, his findings would be the straw that broke the camel's back. Now, he was sure Annie's story of Alvin's infidelity would never hold up.

Chapter Seven
Trial Begins

On September 8, 1927, a carnival-like atmosphere hung over the small river port town of Smithland as if a celebrity had come to town. For six months, the whole county and much of western Kentucky had anticipated this day, and it had finally arrived. At last, the notorious Annie Clemens was going on trial for the murder of her husband, Alvin.

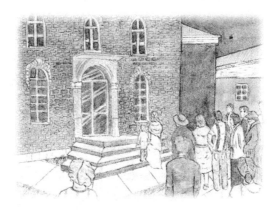

Courthouse Scene

The town was buzzing that bright September morning. Photographers, newspaper reporters, and the local radio station were on hand for the event. Horses and carriages, wagons and T-models lined the street in front of the courthouse.

Summer had not yet lost its simmer and, although the morning began on the cool side, the afternoon would be hot as blue blazes. The sweltering heat only served to fuel their determination. As people filed in, the bailiff announced, "Standing room only." A few more people squeezed their way inside before the tall wooden doors slammed shut. The low rumble of excited voices hushed when the presiding judge entered the courtroom and called the court to order.

Many had come just to get a look at Annie. They strained their necks above the crowd for a peek. She sat next to her lawyer, still just as beautiful as ever. How could someone so lovely have done such a thing?

Six months of tireless preparation had led up to that day. Annie's lawyer had started filing papers for her defense immediately following the murder. First on his agenda was to get Annie's steamer trunk back in her possession. She had demanded he get it for her. Until she got her hands on the letters, she couldn't eat or sleep, and her story would not be credible if they were made public.. Little did she know, her brother-in-law, Lucian, had already opened the trunk and uncovered her secret.

Secondly, he had spent days trying to convince the judge that Annie was not a threat to the community and should be released on bond into her father's custody. He had come up from Florida and was staying nearby at the Heater Hotel. Annie was not used to confinement and jail was driving her crazy.

Third on his list had been to get Annie a fair trial. His argument was that most of the county was bitter and hostile toward the defendant, she being an outsider. In contrast, Alvin was a well-respected man from the Slocum community with numerous friends and relatives, all seeking revenge for the death of an innocent man.

All in all, most of her lawyer's work had been successful. He had gotten Annie's trunk delivered to her within two weeks following her arrest. He also had gotten her released into her father's custody on a $5,000 bond, but the trial, fair or not, would not be moved. He had his work cut out for him.

The prosecution also had its own obstacles to overcome. Because it was a high profile case, it had been virtually impossible to find jury members who hadn't heard or read about the murder. Also, the local paper had run a column just a few days after the incident stating that Annie had said she was beaten by Alvin when she had tried to interfere with him and the young girl. In self-defense, she had armed herself with a shotgun and killed him. True or not, it could have created sympathy for Annie in the minds of the jurors making Alvin's murder, even at the hand of his wife, more understandable. Hopefully, her lawyer could convince the twelve citizens to leave their preconceived ideas at home.

Opening remarks by the prosecution and defense were presented. The defendant's lawyer moved the court to instruct the jury to find Annie "Not Guilty" while the other side asked for "Murder in the First."

One person at a time, the trial proceeded as each witness recanted the events surrounding Alvin's death. Excerpts from those testimonies are now provided for your consideration.

Chapter Eight
Love Letters Read in Court

Since Alvin's brother, Lucian, had discovered the love letters, he was one of the first called by the prosecution to testify. He had been given the distasteful job of reading them to the jury. Regardless of his feelings, he wanted the court to hear them. They would be sure to dismantle Annie's defense.

The letters formed a paper trail of Annie's days in Florida beginning during the winters of 1923 and '24. Ray wrote to her nearly every day. Of course, the jury didn't have Annie's letters to Ray, but the prosecution hoped to show through his letters to her, a woman madly in love. So much so that she would do anything to be with Ray. And, vice versa, he would do anything to be with her.

Lucian began his testimony with the morning of March 17th, the day his brother died and continued until the day he discovered the letters in Annie's trunk. He read them one by one, making no attempt to hide his disgust. It came through loud and clear.

You dear sweet girl . . . It seems like you have been gone a hundred years and it has only been 12 days. If time doesn't begin to pass a little swifter, I'll be as old as Tu-Tank-ha-men (whoever he was) before I see you again. Did I really surprise you when I told you I was crazy about you? It seems like every time you looked at me you couldn't fail to read my secret as if it was written across my face in letters an inch long. If you had not said what you did about being left a widow, I would have driven away without saying a word.

Annie Laurie . . . I'll never forget the first time I ever saw you. It was at Bill's. The thresher was there. We came in for dinner and was washing our faces. You came out on that little porch on the west side of the house, and if someone had cracked me on the head, I could not have felt funnier. Wish I could tell you what queer feelings I had, but I couldn't if I had the vocabulary of Milton or Shakespeare. I asked who you were, and they did not know, so I went to Bill. I knew I could find out from him, and he said, "That is Alvin's Georgia-lady." Then I had some more funny feelings. How do you suppose I felt when I came down there that evening hunting, and you advised me to get a wife instead of a cook? And right then I was looking into the eyes of the only girl I ever saw that I would give two scoops for, and she belonged to someone else.

Annie Laurie, you wonderful girl. You may belong to someone else, but half of my heart is locked against anyone but you with "No Trespass" signs posted around. It is yours whenever you care to enter, but for others "nothing cooking."

"Honey-bunch" don't be afraid to write me anything you want me to know. I will sure be discreet. You can safely trust me.

Because he was mailing a letter to her every day, he knew it would raise suspicion in a small community like Slocum. He did his best to keep them guessing. He began mailing his letters from a different post office every day. That way, it wouldn't be so obvious. With incoming mail, he came up with different ways to trick the post office clerk. He asked Annie to always send it to his post office box number, but to leave off the name. He had talked to a postal worker who had told him that would be okay. Another time, he told her to address it to an anonymous man's name, but to the same box. He tried to think of everything so no one would catch on.

Sweetheart, don't be the least bit uneasy for I have already studied up an explanation. If anyone ever happens to know you ever wrote to me, I'll tell them you were writing giving instructions for making that table, ha, ha. Is that pretty clever or not?

They agreed to exchange pictures the first winter in Florida. He sent her the most recent he had -- a picture of him in his army uniform.

Sweetheart, I mailed you that photograph this morning and I am afraid I hadn't ought to have done it. For you can't keep A. from finding it and causing you trouble maybe. But I can't refuse to do what you ask, so I sent it, and it is up to you to be as careful as possible.

Ray hated the days he didn't get a letter. It seemed like a lifetime since she had left. His love for her was beyond control. He wanted her with all his heart, but not like this. He wanted her for himself. He had never been in love and thought he would go crazy if he couldn't have her.

"Honey Bunch, if I live 400 years, I'll never be able to pay you for the pleasure and happiness you gave me by writing me that letter. Ever since you left, I had been hoping and wondering if you would . . . when your letter came, well, I just had a "fit with a hole in it.""

"Baby Girl . . . I could have bought a hundred turkeys closer to home, but Annie Laurie had the turkeys to sell, and I wanted to see her so why shouldn't I buy from her? Help her get rid of her turkeys and get to see her also . . .."

"Honey Bunch" you're just kidding me when you say you wish I was there, or you was here. If you really meant that, it would be just too good to be true and you "hope I do love you just a little bit?" Sweetheart! I don't love you just a little bit, but I love you so much and have for a hundred years . . . I'm afraid I made a mistake when I told you how dear you were to me. As long as I kept it to myself, it was quiet, like water behind a dam, but when I told you of it, the dam broke. Of course, the flood runs out, not that I think my love for you would ever lose its force, but I mean it is beyond control."

"Oh, Annie Laurie, you lovely girl, if you were only mine and Junior was our boy. That would be everything, nothing else would count . . ."

". . . Do you know I hate for you to come back up here and have to live with anyone else? Before, it didn't seem so bad, but now I can't bear to think of it . . . I love you so well I can't bear to know you have to give up to anyone, but me, or have to go to bed with anyone else . . ."

Ray often called Annie's place, "Little Heaven," because of his love for her and the time they had spent together there. It just wasn't the same without Annie Laurie.

". . . We were going down to your place, Little Heaven, hunting today, but it rained too much, and it is turning colder tonight . . ."

". . . Jesse and me met at George's, and we went down to your place, Little Heaven, and had an excellent time. Found lots of birds and we three got 32 . . ."

Annie had written of trouble between her and Alvin, but Ray couldn't believe that anyone would treat her badly.

"Sweet and lovely and everything that is adored, I don't see how Alvin could turn against you after you've done what you have for him. I've said a dozen times there wasn't many girls that would go to an old "shack" like you did in the place it's in and make a home for a man like you did for him. Some men are lucky and don't know it . . ."

"Honey Girl, You spoke of how Alvin's love seemed to grow cold after Junior came. If I had been in his place and loved you before he came, I would have worshiped you afterwards . . ."

"Baby Girl . . . If Alvin is as jealous as you say, he'll raise cain with you if I come to see you . . . I'll come to see you whenever you say for me to, no matter what he does or says. It will be great if we can be clever and keep him in the dark and never let him catch on. I'll come by going fishing and stop and steal a kiss or two while he's out plowing . . ."

For eighteen months, the affair continued. As their letters reveal, she loved him or made him believe she loved him, as much as he did her.

"Baby Dear . . . you said you loved me better than anything . . . if you was free, you would propose to me . . ."

"Honey Bunch . . . You make a tender feeling well up in my heart for you when you say you would be the happiest girl in the world if you could be with me all the time."

"Dear Annie . . . you have been neglected and unappreciated for so awful long and had no one to tell her troubles to. Sweetheart, it won't always be that way. It is always darkest before dawn, and maybe the dawn is just over the horizon . . ."

"Dearest, as long as we love each other, let us hope that sometime we may be to each other just what we want to be. Our souls joined together as one, shall we continue to hope?"

"Dearest Honey Bunch . . . Your letters made me crazier about you if that was possible. You told me in them that you loved me. It is the first time you've said you love me, and I don't see how I'm ever going to wait until the last of March to see you . . ."

During her last winter in Florida, something changed. Annie's letters became few and far between.

"Honey Bunch, are you sick? It has been one hundred years since I heard from you. I looked for a letter Saturday night, but none came and then I thought surely I'll hear from you Monday, but I didn't, and no letter Tuesday night, and none last night. I've waited as long as I can . . . I am awfully afraid you are real sick . . . Sweetheart, let me hear from you as soon as possible. I can't stand this suspense."

Ray's letters continued even when Annie failed to write. Obviously, he began to have doubts and now he wanted answers.

"Darling girl . . . there is one thing that will make me quit loving you, and that is deceitfulness. I hate deceit worse than anything on earth. Don't care how much you deceive the other fellow, but if you value my love, don't try it on me."

Before she returned home in the spring of 1926, Annie's letters to Ray had stopped altogether. Now, he knew the truth. She never really loved him at all. She had played him for a fool. Surely, he couldn't have been that stupid. He wanted to be wrong. Letter after letter, he tried to persuade her to change her mind.

"Annie Laurie . . . I have wished a thousand times when you have treated me so badly that I did not love you so much, then maybe it would not hurt so much."

"Baby Dear . . . I bet a hundred dollars if you was here you would rather go possum hunting with your Slocum bunch than be with me."

"Baby Girl . . . If only you knew how well I love you and how it hurts me to have you act like you don't care for me. Surely you would either learn to love me better or be honest and tell me my little dream is over, and you would rather not see me anymore."

"Baby Girl . . . I go to sleep as soon as I "hit the hay" and wake up in about two hours and lay there the rest of the night thinking about you and how dark my future looked at present. Oh! If your love had only proved true . . ."

He was hurt and angry. Obviously, she had only used him. He blamed Annie for leading him on, but he blamed himself most of all for falling in love with a married woman in the first place. How could he have been so stupid?

". . . You remember last summer when you would treat me so bad I would tell you that you was widening the gulf between us? You did not seem to care, at least, you did not try to help things but kept on and on until you made a skeptic out of me as far as your love for me was concerned. A fellow can go too far sometimes . . ."

". . . You say you have longed to be with me so many times since you left. If you had longed to be with me a little before you left, I might believe that . . ."

". . . I've caught you in a fib . . . went over to Wee Willie's Saturday and she had a letter from you. Said you had landed a job in a real estate office down there and was busy as a bird dog in a stubble field. You couldn't tell me the truth on a bet . . . when I look back and see how you've done, I realize that only a fool would ever have believed in you and trusted and loved you like I have . . ."

Sometime during the course of their affair, Annie told Ray she had an illness of a private nature and tried to put the blame on him. He had to know if he was the one to blame.

"Baby girl, You spoke of consulting a doctor, and he told you that you were in a pretty bad fix. What did he say was wrong? I think I am entitled to know for you said, or as much as said, I was responsible for your condition, that you had given up to me so much was the cause. I won't say that I am, for I don't know, but I do know you have given up to me 78 times between 18 and 19 months which is a little more than four times a month which doesn't seem to be often enough to injure you."

He's nearly crazy. No matter what, there is no way he can give her up.

"Baby girl, I love you, loved you, and I'll never stop loving you as long as I live, no matter what you do. I could no more stop loving you than I could stop breathing."

"Oh you sweet baby girl, hurry and come home, won't you please and make me happy once in life and, at the same time, as miserable as anyone can be, for sweetheart after holding your precious self in my arms and loving and kissing you, how can I ever give you up to another?"

After being in Florida for a while, Annie decided she wanted to move there, so she tried to persuade Ray to buy some land in the sunshine state.

". . . So you want to sell me a lot, do you? Do you really think it is a good buy? If I bought it, I wouldn't want to resell. I would want to keep it to live on someday if I ever have anyone to love me enough to say, "Yes, I'll cook your pota-toes." Do you know anyone who would like to live with me in Tampa Beach?"

". . . If I had enough to buy a nice place in Florida, noth-ing would make me any happier than to do so and take you to it and spend the rest of my life trying to make you happy . . ."

After all her persuading, Ray doesn't buy the Florida property. At this point, Annie changes her strategy and, once again, puts the blame on him.

"Baby girl, You said you begged me to take you away from here, but I would not. Sweetheart, Don't you know why I didn't? There was two good reasons. Mother and Jun-ior. Think it over. I could hardly leave her in her condition, and I just couldn't take you away from your boy. If we could move and take him with us, it would be different. If I had taken you away from him, after awhile, when I would have come in and caught you crying and know you were crying for him, I couldn't bear it knowing I was the cause of your unhappiness . . . You asked me if I blamed you for not want-ing to live here any longer under the present circumstances. No, I can't blame you at all. I believe a fellow ought to make living as pleasant for his wife as it is possible for him to and if he don't love her or she him, and they can't get along without quarreling, it is time to quit."

Twenty-seven letters and several hours later, the mood of the entire courtroom changed. If there was ever any doubt about Annie's unscrupulous reputation, the letters had erased it all.

Linda C. DeFew

Chapter Nine
Alvin's Letters to Annie

In addition to Ray's letters, Alvin also wrote letters to Annie while they were apart. Before they questioned her, she was asked to read those incriminating letters to the court. Annie was at a huge disadvantage in a couple of ways. To begin with, the majority of her letters to her husband were not accounted for because Alvin didn't keep all of them. Also, she said a bundle of her letters to him had been stolen out of her trunk while out of her possession, but she could not prove it. So, we have to ascertain from Alvin's letters what had been said in Annie's letters to him. The following letter was written thirteen months before Alvin's death, and we can assume the marriage was in big trouble.

". . . I am in a bum little old hotel, and it is pouring rain and turning cold, and I can't even get out of the house to walk and try to find something to occupy my mind. Came an awful rain storm here last night and the thunder and lightning just made the house tremble and the rain just poured, but the rain that poured from the sky was no more copious than the tears that gushed from my eyes and soaked my pillow. You have torn the very heart out of my breast, and if I could only lay down and die, I would feel that it would be

one of God's greatest blessings. You have wrecked all my plans of life and have shattered every air castle I have built for the future . . . I am perfectly wild and nearly insane . . . You know how I love Jr., and you know too how he loved me and then to tear him away from me in this manner is the meanest thing in this world that you could possibly do to me. I can never forget the last goodbye to Jr., when he brought that old lap spread out to me at the hack the day I left and I can see the big tears trickle down his sweet cheeks and the few minutes I held him on my lap crushed to my heart before I drove away were moments I can never forget."

In the second letter, Alvin tried to find out why Annie didn't tell him earlier about her plans to leave.

" . . . Now, Annie Laurie, if you meant to take out, why didn't you come clean and tell me so before you left so I could have made changes then accordingly? I would not have bought the cream separator, would not have killed and put up $75 worth of meat, would not have kept and wintered all those chickens and turkeys, would not have wintered all that stock and fed high-priced food and paid Dock to feed them . . . If a woman loves a man, she can be happy with him any place, and she can either be a big help to him in getting along, or she can tie his hands so he can't get along just as

she prefers to do. Now, if you don't want to spend your life in Slocum, I would not ask you to as there is lots of places to live besides there and there are lots of schools to send a boy to, but you are not playing on the level . . . Our affairs are not in a shape just now to tear up without a big loss. The time to do that kind of planning is in the fall, and we should talk it over together and come to an understanding and work together unless you just want to turn me loose and to paddle your own boat. Then if that is your desire, things would have to be figured different and so far as you taking charge of Jr., and me having no son at all -- well, that would have to be decided by someone other than you or myself and don't think that I would not make a desperate effort and I might dig up some things buried in the past, some that your own mother would not know.

The third letter related his plans of quitting his job as a salesman and coming home.

" . . . If you will not come back, well, I am going to be there anyway, but as to what I would or would not do, I could not even give you the shadow of an idea, as I don't know. I would be like a ship without a sail."

" . . . I will feel free to arrange my affairs there (Slocum) and say goodbye to the old home of my childhood . . . I feel

duty bound to see that he (dad) and mama are taken care of and will not be willing to leave them . . . my future looks very dark and dreary, and most of all this trip have been very miserable for me just from the letters you wrote or from the ones you never did write that I looked for and called time after time for only to be turned away in sadness."

The court heard the words of a man at the lowest ebb of his life, a man destroyed by the woman he loved. If only she hadn't saved his letters, Annie's story might have been more credible. Now, her whole case was falling apart.

Chapter Ten
Annie's Testimony

The first few hours of Annie's testimony was spent covering her family history, her formative years growing up in Quitman, Georgia, and her relationship with her parents. Everything seemed perfectly normal up until the day she ran away from home to be with Alvin.

Annie Called to Testify

She said she fell in love with him while on a temporary job in Illinois. Weeks after she arrived back home in Georgia, he called her to go on the road with him. She said she knew her parents would object, so she left without telling them. She called later to inform them of their marriage, and they told her not to come back home.

She recounted the birth of their child, Junior, and their move to Kentucky. When asked about Alvin's employment, she stated that he farmed full time for the first few years, but in the fall of 1923, he accepted a job with *Jell-O* as a traveling salesman. For the next four years, he worked for the company, leaving home in the fall and returning in the spring. It was during those winters that she and Junior went to visit with her family in their new home in Florida.

When he was gone, she and her husband corresponded almost every day. She kept his letters, brought them back home with her, and locked them in her trunk. Not until the winter of 1926 thru '27, had Alvin varied from his normal routine, taking a shorter route. She told the jury that Alvin left home the first day of January and came home February 22, shortly after submitting his resignation.

Everyone gave Annie their full attention when the lawyers began questioning her about Ray. They asked if Alvin knew about her affair with his good friend and about the letters they had written each other. Annie said he knew all about their affair and said she had done no worse than he had, so they forgave each other and put the whole thing behind them. She claimed he wasn't angry with her and they never argued. However, many found it hard to believe that Alvin had asked her to keep Ray's letters, along with the ones she had received from him, in her trunk. Nevertheless, she said he promised her that when he got his financial matters in order, he would take her and Junior and leave Slocum.

She went on to testify about the night of the killing and stated that she, Alvin, and Junior all went inside, undressed in the parlor (north room) where it was warm, and went upstairs to sleep. She was awakened around 2:00 a.m. by Ruby, who told her that Alvin had sent her up there. When she got downstairs, she saw Sylvia in Alvin's arms, and the next thing she knew, he was lying on the floor. She told Sylvia to call her father.

The following is part of her testimony concerning her relationship with her husband:

Q. Tell the jury whether or not your husband knew about these letters that you received from Raymond?

A. He did.

Q. Your husband, Alvin, knew about those letters you had in that trunk from Raymond?

A. Yes, sir.

Q. Tell in what way he knew about them?

A. I had showed them to him.

Q. Tell the jury whether or not your husband knew about the photograph of Raymond Baker that you had, which was introduced by the Commonwealth?

A. He did.

Q. Tell the jury when you showed the photograph of Ray and the letters you had received from Ray to your husband.

A. After he returned in the spring.

Q. Which spring, do you mean 1927?

A. 1926.

Q. Tell where it was and what passed between you.

A. We were in our home in Slocum.

Q. Tell all about it?

A. After the two letters that were read (in court), we had come to a better understanding and I wrote and told him I was coming back, and when I got back home, I told him that I had not been doing as I ought to and he wanted to know what I had been doing, and I told him about having these letters and this picture of Ray, and he wanted to see them, and I showed them to him, and he said to me, "You have done no worse than I have done." He had asked if he could see the letters and I said, 'yes." I was willing for him to see them.

Q. What then?

A. After he read them, I asked him about giving them back to Ray and he said "no" for me to keep the picture and the letters both.

Q. What did he say about putting them in the trunk?

A. He was there when I put them in the trunk; he saw me do it. He told me to.

Q. Did you tell your husband about your relations with Ray?

A. I did.

Q. Tell what he said about that?

A. He said, "Well, you haven't done any worse than I have done," and he said that the best thing to do on account of our boy was to forgive each other.

Q. Tell what was said about a change of location?

A. I wanted Junior to have a good school, and I also wanted to leave there and he told me that when he got his matters straightened up that we would leave. He promised me he would leave.

Q. State whether or not he told you of the things he had been guilty of?

A. He did.

Q. What did he say about that?

A. He said he had not been living as he should on the road. He said he had visited the "red-light" districts.

Q. Tell whether or not after this agreement your husband went back on the road for another short time?

A. He did, in 1927.

Q. At the time you showed him the letters you had from Ray, did you also show your husband the letters you had received from him, about which you have testified about?

A. I did.

Q. What did he say?

A. He wanted me to put them all together, and he wanted me to keep the letters for awhile and asked me to keep his and Ray's letters together for awhile.

Q. Did you and your husband ever quarrel?

A. No, sir.

Q. State whether or not you were angry with your husband or he with you at the time you talked over these letters and had this agreement?

A. No sir, we were not.

Q. Tell whether or not your husband gave you any advice about how to keep the letters a secret in the community?

A. I asked him what to do, and he told me to keep them for awhile. He said no one knows about it, but us. He said, just keep them awhile.

Q. Is that all that passed between you that time?

A. It is with the exception of telling each other what we had done, and we forgave each other and we were happy.

Q. Did you continue to live together as husband and wife?

A. It is, and we were happy.

Q. Tell what the relationship was between you and your husband after that time?

A. We were happy together, and we lived as man and wife should.

Q. Now, when you went downstairs into the hall, tell what you saw?

A. When I got to the door, I looked in the room. In the room there I saw him in bed with Sylvia. I seen her in his arms and I don't know of anything else.

Q. Tell what the next thing was you realized?

A. The next thing I realized was I think Sylvia screamed.

Q. And then what was the next thing you saw?

A. I saw Alvin laying on the floor.

Q. Tell what you did?

A. I told Sylvia to call somebody.

Q. Did she call?

A. She went to the telephone and rang.

Q. Did she get anyone to come?

A. She called, but I don't remember whether the party she called came or not.

Q. Tell what you did next?

A. We left the room and went out in the hall, and I called Ruby. She was upstairs and she came downstairs, and we all went out the back door together.

Q. How were you clothed -- you and the other ladies?

A. We had our night clothes on.

Q. Where did you go then?

A. Went down to the gate. (She states that the mail-boxes were located down there too, about 65 to 70 ft. of the house.)

Q. Do you remember what you did when you got out to the mailbox?

A. Met two boys.

Q. Who were they?

A. Turk Trail and Herman Ferrell.

Q. Is that the same Turk Trail that testified before the jury, in this case, the other day?

A. Yes, sir.

Q. What took place then?

A. I asked him if Mr. Adams was coming and he said, "No," that Ora Suits and Odell were coming down the road.

Q. Which Adams were you inquiring about?

A. Harrison Adams.

Q. Who were the next parties who arrived after Turk Trail and the Ferrell boys got there?

A. Odell Adams and Ora Suits.

Q. Where were you and Ruby and Sylvia when Adams and Suits arrived there?

A. Half way between the mailbox and the culvert.

Q. Still clothed in your night clothing?

A. Yes, sir.

Q. What occurred?

A. When we got down there, I heard somebody coming up the road, and I walked down to the culvert just a few feet.

Q. What direction did they come from?

A. From the direction of Harrison Adams.

Q. Were Suits and Adams over at the dance at Harrison Adams' that night?

A. Yes, sir.

Q. When the Adams boy and the Suits boy came up, tell what happened?

A. I heard them talking and recognized their voices and said, "Ora, is that you?" And he said, "What is the matter?" and I said, "I have shot Alvin."

Q. What happened then, did you go back to the house?

A. Yes, sir.

Q. Who went to the house?

A. Ruby, Sylvia and myself, Ora, Orville Adams.

Q. Did anybody go in the house?

A. Yes, sir.

Q. Who?

A. Ora Suits.

Q. What room did he go in?

A. North room.

Q. At that time, did you go back to the house?

A. We went back to the house together.

Q. Who came next?

A. Mr. George Kimsey and Finis Pugh.

Q. Do you know what time of morning it was this occurred?

A. I couldn't say for sure.

Q. Can you give an idea about what time in the morning it was?

A. I should judge between two and three o'clock.

Q. On the occasion of this killing, did you and your husband have any words?

A. No, sir, we did not.

Q. Had you had any words that day or that night?

A. No, sir.

Q. Had you ever quarreled?

A. No, sir.

Q. What sort of weather was it on the occasion?

A. It had been raining. It wasn't raining that night. It was awfully muddy though.

Q. Was it a dark or light night?

A. It was a bright moonlight night.

Q. Did you intend to kill your husband?

A. I did not.

Q. Tell what you did when you realized that your husband had been shot.

A. I was torn almost to pieces.

Annie was cross-examined over and over, but stuck tightly to her story -- she shot her husband in the heat of the moment. A crime of passion was understandable in her eyes -- if only those people would understand.

Annie had no answer for the large and small impressions in the featherbed downstairs, but she gave a reasonable explanation for the window screen being torn. She said she had washed windows the week before and pulled the screen down just enough to put her hand inside. She had just neglected to fix it back when she finished.

When questioned about the rumors of her affair with Ray, she says it was over with him. Also, she denied having a private conversation with him the afternoon before the murder.

Q. When was it that you and Ray first commenced to have an affair?

A. We started our correspondence the winter I went to Palmetto, Florida.

Q. Who wrote the first letter?

A. I did.

Q. What year?

A. In the fall of '23.

Q. You were in love with him?

A. No, sir.

Q. Why were you writing him?

A. Just before I left home, he came to my house and bought some turkeys and he asked me when I was leaving and I told him tomorrow, and he wanted to know if I would try to find him a girl and I said, "yes." And I asked him if he wanted to find a widow, and he said he wanted a red-headed girl and I said "all right," I would see if I could find him one.

Q. That is the reason you wrote him?

A. Yes, sir.

Q. Did he tell you he loved you when you were down there?

A. He didn't exactly say he loved me. He said he was crazy about me.

Q. And after that, you all corresponded?

A. Yes, sir.

Q. Did you ever write that you were in love with him?

A. I don't just remember now the things which I wrote him.

Q. Did you at any time love him?

A. I thought I did at one time.

She explained that she had become intimate with Ray the summer following her return from her first trip to Florida in 1924 and that the affair continued until she left again in the fall of 1925.

Q. Now, when was it, that you and your husband had this talk together in which you told him of the letters that you had received from Ray?

A. It was in the spring of 1926 after we returned home.

Q. Did you tell your husband you had been intimate with Ray?

A. Yes, sir.

Q. And he didn't get mad?

A. No, sir.

Q. Did you tell him over how long a period that continued?

A. I did.

Q. He didn't get mad at that?

A. No, sir.

Q. Did he read all his letters?

A. Yes, sir.

Q. Did you see Ray after you returned to Slocum in the spring of 1926?

A. I did, but after I came back, I had no more to do with him.

Q. Now after the conversation between you and your husband and your agreement to go on and live and forgive and forget, you didn't flirt with any other men?

A. I did not.

Q. Did he?

A. No.

Q. You didn't make a date with Orville Adams just before your husband was killed?

A. I did not.

Q. You didn't talk to him on the phone?

A. I did not.

The questioning moved to the night of the murder.

Q. Ruby came upstairs and told you that Alvin had run her out of bed and had told her to come up and get in bed with you?

A. Yes, sir.

Q. And she did that?

A. Yes, sir.

Q. Then what did you do?

A. I didn't say anything to Ruby. I got up and went downstairs.

Q. Immediately?

A. Yes, sir.

Q. Walked downstairs to the end of the hallway?

A. Yes, sir.

Q. What else?

A. I walked to the north room (parlor) door.

Q. What did you see?

A. I saw him in bed with Sylvia.

Q. Sylvia say anything?

A. When I was coming down the steps, I heard her scream.

Q. He was in bed with her?

A. Yes, sir.

Q. Could you tell what position?

A. I don't know as I could.

Q. Then what happened?

A. I don't remember.

Q. You don't remember?

A. I don't remember what happened.

Q. What was the next thing you remembered?

A. Sylvia screamed.

Q. Where were you then?

A. Standing in the room.

Q. Inside the room?

A. Yes.

Q. Have a gun in your hand?

A. No, sir.

Q. Where was the gun?

A. I couldn't say. I don't know what I did with it.

Q. When did you next see it?

A. Not until they brought it up here yesterday.

Q. When you were standing in the room and heard Sylvia scream, where was your husband?

A. Lying on the floor.

Q. How far from the bed?

A. Lying at the foot of the bed.

Q. His head or feet towards the bed?

A. I don't remember.

Q. Was Sylvia still in bed?

A. No, sir. She had gotten out of bed.

The questioning continued, going over the same incidents time and time again. Only one thing had changed in her testimony -- immediately following the shooting, she had blurted out the fact that she had shot Alvin. Many witnesses testified to that fact. But, later, she said she didn't remember anything from the time she saw Alvin in bed with Sylvia to the time she saw him lying on the floor dead. Why had she altered her story?

Linda C. DeFew

Chapter Eleven
Ruby & Sylvia Testify

The Clemens' neighbor, Ruby, age 15, took the stand after Annie. Ruby had been staying with the Clemens' family since Alvin left on January 1, up until the time of his death on March 17. Since that time, she had married a local boy, Alvin King.

When asked about the events leading up to the murder, she said that she and her friend, Sylvia, walked home from the dance with Annie, Alvin, and Junior, along with a couple of boyfriends. They were allowed to stay out on the porch for about thirty minutes with the boys. Afterward, they retired to their bed in the parlor. She hadn't been asleep long before Alvin woke her up and told her to go sleep with Annie. She hurried upstairs and told Annie, but Annie said nothing. She simply got up and went downstairs. Ruby said she climbed into Annie's bed and went back to sleep immediately. The next thing she heard was the sound of Sylvia screaming. She said she never heard a gunshot.

When asked about the window screen, Ruby explained that Ora Suits was working on the Clemens' phone line on

Monday before the murder and pulled the screen loose at that time. Later, she said that she and Annie tore it when they were washing windows earlier in the week.

She was asked if she knew of Annie's extramarital affairs, particularly the latest one with Orville. Ruby said she didn't know about any affairs. She explained that Orville had been to the Clemens' house several times, but since she and Orville were cousins, he came to visit her, not Annie.

Sylvia, age 18, took the stand after Ruby. She had never been in the Clemens' house before that night. She gave the same account up until the point where she was awakened. She says Alvin had laid down beside her and asked her to "give him something." She screamed, and he jumped out of bed and crossed over to the dresser. Sylvia then turned on her side facing the wall and started to cry. She hadn't much more than got herself turned when the gun fired. She said Annie rushed into the dark room and quickly lit the lamp. Then, she walked out in the hall with Annie and returned to the parlor when she told her to call for help. Oddly enough, she said she didn't see Alvin's body anywhere in the room.

After walking to the bridge and meeting the boys, she said she stayed at the bridge while the others went back to the house to see if Alvin was dead. Later, she said that when

Ora came out of the house, he said, "Annie, you have shot him, and he is dead, and there isn't any use to story about it."

When asked about the events at the dance, Sylvia said Annie danced her last dance with Orville. Afterward, she said she overheard Orville ask another lady if he could borrow a pistol saying he wanted to see what Alvin would do about him dancing with Annie.

After the girls' testimony, other witnesses were called, contradicting what Ruby and Sylvia had said in court compared to what they had said to them in private. "Annie threatened my life if I didn't swear like I did that day Alvin lay a corpse," said Sylvia to one witness. To another, she said, "Annie should go to the electric chair for killing her husband, Alvin." Away from the courtroom, Ruby also admitted that Annie had threatened both of them to the point of fearing for their lives.

In regard to Annie's relationship with Ray, numerous people said that Sylvia had told them that Annie and Ray had engaged in a private conversation the afternoon before the murder. It had taken place when Annie and Ruby had gone to see Ray's bedridden mother. A number of visitors were present when Annie got up and left the house with Ray. After about thirty minutes, Annie came back in and told Sylvia to come home with them and go to the dance that night. Sylvia told her that her parents wouldn't let her go, but Annie would not take "no" for an answer. Otherwise, Sylvia would not have been at the Clemens' house that night at all.

Chapter Twelve
Ora & Orville's Testimony

Ora Suits, a lifelong resident of Slocum, testified that he had only known Annie for about four years, but had known Alvin all his life. He worked for the local telephone company and had been called upon to do repair work on the Clemens' telephone a few days before Alvin's death. He said he was at the dance the night of the killing and stayed until it broke up about 2:00 a.m. As he and his friend, Odell, were walking home, he said he heard a "crying racket" coming from the front of the Clemens' house.

He hollered and asked what was the matter?

Mrs. Clemens yelled, "Ora, is that you?"

"What's the matter?" Ora asked.

"Run here quick. I have shot Alvin."

He said they ran to meet Annie, Ruby, and Sylvia at the concrete bridge just a few yards from Annie's house. Hoping he had misunderstood, he asked again, "What did you say?"

"I have shot Alvin," Annie said distinctly.

Ora couldn't believe it. "You don't mean to say you have done a thing like that. What made you do a thing like that?"

"I couldn't help it. I had to," Annie replied.

He asked if they had called a doctor and they said, "No." He asked if the man was dead. They said they didn't know if he was dead or not, so Ora insisted they go back to the house and find out.

About that time, Orville Adams jumped the fence into the road and asked what all the excitement was about. Ora told him what Annie had said. Then, Ora, Orville, Odell, Sylvia, and Annie went to the house, but only he and Orville went inside. Ora stated that the front hall door going into the parlor was closed, but he could see a light burning through the crack at the bottom. The following is Ora's description in his own words of what he found when he opened the door:

"Alvin's feet were laying just inside of the door. In going through the door, you had to go around his head to keep from stepping on him; his head was also laying toward the bed which was located in the corner against the same wall into which the door is built. He was lying on his face with his left hand under his body and to his body, like that (Indicating.) In his right hand was a towel, it looked to be."

Ora then stopped in the door, turned around to Orville and said, "He is just as dead as he can be." He then proceeded to walk over to Alvin and put his hand down to his left side to feel for his heartbeat, but there wasn't any. He felt for his pulse and didn't feel any there. He told Orville to bring the others back to the house because the man was dead.

Ora was asked if he saw a gun the day he was called to work on the Clemens' telephone. He said Mrs. Clemens went outside with a gun, shot some birds in a tree, then, took it back in the house.

Much questioning was done regarding the detour Orville took on the way home from the dance to the bridge just above the Clemens' place. Ora said Orville had told him he was going to the Suits' barn to get a hame string for his horse. After about fifteen minutes, he caught up with them at the bridge where he heard the commotion.

Next, the lawyer dropped a bombshell when he asked Ora if on December 21, 1923, he went to Dr. Masoncup for an examination and if the doctor issued to him a signed certificate. He handed the paper, signed by the doctor, to him for verification:

Letter in Tree

Lola, KY

December 21, 1923

To whom it may concern:

This is to certify that I have this day examined Ora Suits for specific or private disease of the genito-urinary organs, and do not find any indications of any disease.

Signed,

Charles Masoncup

Realizing where this line of questioning was headed, Ora denied everything. He said he had never had improper relations with the defendant, but it doesn't take him long to recant his story. The lawyer told the court that the certificate had been found in Annie's trunk where she kept all things of a personal nature. Ora knew there was no way he could convince the jury that he hadn't given it to her, so he came clean. He said their affair started by writing letters to each other and using an old tree on her farm for a post office. She mailed letters to him by placing them in a hole in the tree, and he did likewise. He assured the court that the affair had been over for some time.

Next to testify, Orville Adams, age 20, born and raised in Slocum. Like Ora, he had known Alvin all his life but had only known Annie since Alvin brought her to Kentucky. He was asked about his whereabouts after leaving the dance. He said that he, his brother, Odell, and Ora all left together around 1:00 a.m. to go home. Along the way, Orville said, when they passed the Suits' property, he left the other two boys, cut through the field and ran to their barn to get a hame string for his horse. He caught up with them down the road somewhere close to the concrete bridge, just a few yards from the Clemens' property. Orville said it was there that they heard the girls. Then, he went to the house to check on

Alvin, went for the doctor and didn't arrive back until after daylight.

In previous testimony, one witness stated that Orville had asked him for a pistol at the dance that night because Alvin had objected to his dancing with his wife. He said he was going to do something about it. Orville denied it ever happened.

When asked about his relationship with Annie, he first said that he had never had anything to do with Annie. When the lawyer brought up the testimony of another witness who said otherwise, Orville admitted he only lied in court because he didn't want his wife to know. He said he had been with Annie sexually six times during the winter of '27 while Alvin was out of town. He said she had given him two presents on his birthday -- a shirt with his initials on it and a cake.

He was questioned about an incident that occurred after Alvin got back that past February. According to neighbors, Orville's gray mule was tied across the road from Annie's house, and he was seen going in and staying several hours while Alvin was gone to help a neighbor. He answered that question by saying he was there to visit his cousin, Ruby.

By the time the questioning of these critical witnesses

were over, the jury had not one, but two more men who may have wanted to do away with Alvin.

Linda C. DeFew

Chapter Thirteen
Plea for Insanity

Two doctors from Western State Hospital were called to testify as to Annie's mental state. The defense, in an effort to free their client, had hoped to make it simple. A "crime of passion" was a perfectly reasonable explanation for seeing one's husband in bed with another woman. But, in order to counteract the letters' effect on the jury, they would have to go a step further if they hoped to free their client. A new theory was introduced. Was it possible that Annie had pulled the trigger, but had been temporarily insane?

After lengthy questioning by both sides, one doctor said, "It was an insane act, but he could not say she was insane. He later said he believed the defendant was "functionally insane." This was his logic:

"She was aroused from a deep and profound sleep, having been to the dance the evening before and before a recovery and due to a normal mental condition, she goes down after hearing a report that shocks her to confirm the report that is given to her by the girl that came up to her room and reports her husband's conduct. After she goes down, she is further shocked by the fact that a gun is set by and a suggestion to a partially recovered memory, she acts upon it in a subconscious way and kills her husband. This is based on the same condition exactly as a case of fever or pneumonia."

His conclusion was that "her mind was not normal at the time of the shooting. She probably did not have judgment enough to know between right and wrong."

The second doctor, having heard the whole story, also said Annie is insane, in his opinion. The prosecution asked, "Does that mean that everybody is "insane" if awaken out of sleep and shoots an intruder?" He didn't respond, but admitted that "with the cases he has studied, most all people who killed while insane, killed the people they wanted to kill or get rid of." Insane or not, this final statement destroyed Annie's last ditch effort for freedom.

Chapter Fourteen
The Verdict

At that point in Livingston County history, the "Clemens' vs. State of Kentucky trial went down as the longest and most expensive trial ever to be held in Smithland. However, once the testimony was in, the jury wasted no time in finding Annie guilty of involuntary manslaughter. On September 15, 1927, she was sentenced to eighteen years of hard labor at the state penitentiary in Frankfort, but would only serve twelve. Her lawyers immediately filed a motion for a new trial. Twenty-one breaches of proper court procedure were cited. All their efforts were denied.

No one was really surprised by the verdict. Numerous witnesses had taken the stand on Alvin's behalf. To them, his character was beyond reproach while Annie's was just short of reprobate. Whether she had actually pulled the trigger or not, she was guilty in one way or another.

Of course, everyone knew there was more to it. The prosecution searched for answers to one discrepancy after another. Annie had told three different stories about what actually happened. In the first one, she said she met the boys at the bridge and told them she had just shot her husband. Second, she told the court she couldn't remember what had happened between seeing Alvin with Sylvia in bed together and seeing him dead on the parlor floor. And third, she reported to the county paper that she had shot Alvin after he had beaten her for interfering with his sexual rendezvous.

Through the love letters, the prosecution had attempted to show the jury how Annie premeditated to get rid of her husband to be with another man, but that was impossible to prove. The man who wrote 27 love letters to her and pledged his undying love was never called to the stand. How did Ray avoid having to testify? Some say it was because he was so well respected in the community. Others say that he was in good standing with the Masons and his Masonic brothers shielded him from public embarrassment. Although never brought out in court, one neighbor swore that he saw Ray's horse fly by the Clemens' house shortly after the murder. In light of all the evidence against him, not a soul dared question Ray's absence in court. Undoubtedly, his testimony would have cast new light on a case already shrouded in mystery.

Also, there's the matter of Ora. If he was the one who tore the window screen, was it for the purpose of fixing the phone or was there a more sinister motive behind it? After the shooting, why did he appear on the concrete bridge just as the women came down the road for help? And, if Annie had already told Ora, "I have shot Alvin," why did he tell her not to "story" about it after going in and finding him dead? Now, let's consider Orville's statements. He had tried to make Alvin mad at the dance that very night by dancing with his wife. He boasted of his plan to borrow a pistol to use on the jealous man saying, he was "going to do something about it." Then, on his way home, he decided to go to a man's barn in the middle of the night to get a hame string at precisely the same time of the shooting. And, as if that wasn't enough, he admits to a sexual affair with Annie beginning in January 1927, just before Alvin returned.

Now, let's turn our attention to the girls who were spending the night at the Clemens' house, Ruby and Sylvia. As each girl took the witness stand, we are left to decide on our own what is truth, what is not, and what lies in between. But, we are sure of one thing -- Annie put the fear of God in the two girls. Friends and neighbors remember their parents taking extra care to guard and protect their daughters during and after the trial. Could it be they knew too much? No amount of pressure applied by the prosecution ever got them to change their story.

As far as Annie goes, was she the type of person who would crumble upon seeing her husband in bed with another woman or was she a strong, smart woman with a well-thought-out plan? She immediately took the blame for the shooting but then said she didn't remember shooting her husband due to the shock of seeing him in another woman's arms. What had changed since the day she signed her confession? Had someone convinced her that a memory lapse would set her free to live out her life with her son? And, if nothing else proves her ability to lie on the stand, her answer to one question says it all.

"Did you and your husband ever quarrel?" the lawyer asked.

"No, sir," she answered.

Think about it. Can any couple, after being married 11 years, make that claim?

Epilogue

Two years after I had handed out copies of "Murder in Little Heaven," to my closest friends and relatives, a car drove up in our circle driveway. A middle-aged woman and an elderly man got out as I walked out on the front porch to greet them. They introduced themselves as Truman Williams, age, 90, and his daughter, Helen Watson.

"Are you the lady who wrote the book?" he asked.

"Yes, I am," I replied, not sure if it was an accusation or a compliment.

"I have something I have to tell you," he said in a serious tone.

"Of course. Please have a seat." It was difficult to read his weathered face. Had I stepped on someone's toes? Maybe I had written something that offended him or his family.

He sat down in a rocking chair, and I pulled mine up close to his. His voice was soft but very distinguished and articulate.

"You've got everything exactly right," he stated. "It's

115

all just like I remember it."

I breathed a sigh of relief, realizing I had misread his expression. The last thing I ever wanted to do was offend someone. Instead, it was as if I had paved the road for him to finally release what his conscience had hidden for a lifetime.

He began by telling me that he was only 15 at the time of the murder, but it had left such an impression on him, he remembered it just like it was yesterday. He closed his eyes as if the whole scene was playing out in front of him.

"The day after the murder, all the community was buzzing with the news. All the men in the small community were going down to the Clemens' house. My father had decided to allow me to become a man, to actually go along with him. When I got there, the coroner's jury was waiting in the foyer just outside the room where Alvin lay. I stood in the background as the parlor door was opened, giving me a perfect view of Alvin's body. He was on his stomach with his face pressed solidly into the wood floor. I watched as they carefully turned him over. Rigor mortis had set in, so Alvin's hand fell away just enough to reveal the silver-dollar-size hole in his chest. Only a small amount of blood pooled on the floor, leaving many of them to question if he had been killed somewhere else and moved to his present location. I'll never forget it," he said, shaking his head.

"I can understand that, Mr. Williams. I am so glad you came by to share it with me," I said with all sincerity.

"But wait," he added. "That's not what I came to tell you."

Now, I was really intrigued. His first-hand account was the best I could have hoped for. "Please continue," I said, anxious to hear the whole story.

"Okay," he said. "I have a question. Did you ever figure out who the old man was who came to visit you?"

"No, we never did."

"Well, I do."

"You do?" His eyes told me he meant every word.

"About three days after Alvin was buried, I was walking down the road in front of the Clemens' property. About that time, Alvin's father, Ursh, as his friends called him, drove up in front of his son's house in a hack, tied his horse to a post, and started for the front door."

"How are you doing, Uncle Ursh?" I hollered.

"Very well," he replied solemnly.

"I could tell Mr. Clemens was feeling pretty low, so I followed him into the house. It was one small way I felt I could help. I watched as he stood in the foyer and looked into each room. 'So many things,' he said, staring sadly into the parlor. He crossed the foyer and looked into the kitchen, 'so many things,' the grieving father repeated."

"Now, this is the part that made the hair stand up on my neck," Mr. Williams said. "He walked to the front door, took out his gold pocket watch from his vest, flipped it open, and said one more time, 'So many things . . . remind me of Alvin. I must go now, son,' he said to me as he walked out the door and back to the hack."

I sat there motionless, hardly believing what I was hearing. Goosebumps were popping out across my skin in 90 degree weather. I could feel what he was describing since I had been a part of a similar encounter only a few years ago. Was he thinking the same thing I was?

Overwhelmed with emotion, Mr. Williams looked at me, his eyes filled with tears. He took a few seconds to compose himself, took a deep breath and continued. "The man you described in your story, everything from his actions, to how you said he was dressed, to his gold pocket watch, fit him to a tee. The man you saw was Alvin's father, Mr. Francis Usher Clemens." Having finished what he came to tell me, he stood and told his daughter he was ready to go.

Still in shock, I thanked him for coming and told them to come back anytime. As they drove away, I hurried back to my bedroom, my heart racing in my chest. "There's no way," I said, searching for the box containing all the bits and pieces of research we had put together over the past few years. Could Mr. Williams be right? Then, I found the obituary:

"On the morning of April 25, 1930, the death angel appeared in our midst and claimed for his victim, Francis Usher Clemens, one of the oldest citizens of the Carrsville section."

The fading piece of newspaper would only prove one thing -- the man Mr. Williams said had visited Eddie and me in 1995, had been dead 65 years at the time. He died three years after his son.

THE END

Linda C. DeFew

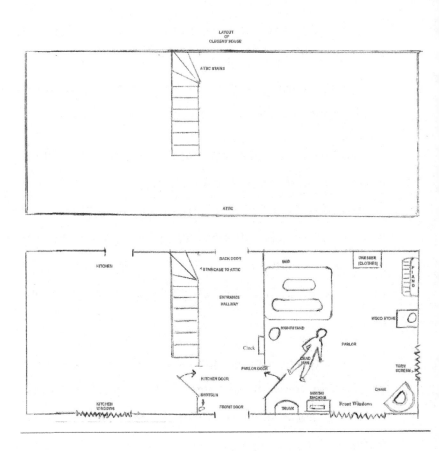

Drawing Based on Trial Testimonies

ABOUT THE AUTHOR

Linda C. Defew lives on a farm in Livingston County, Kentucky, with her husband, Eddie, in the Slocum community. They raise fox terriers, Nubian goats, and a variety of chickens.

Struck with crippling rheumatoid arthritis in her 30's, Linda was forced to leave her job and her love of needlework due to joint damage in her hands. Luckily, her love of writing surfaced after going back to college. With a few adaptions, she was able to type again using one hand.

Today, Linda calls the stories she writes her "therapy," something that takes her mind off of her disease and an uncertain future. During the 15 years she spent researching "Murder in Little Heaven," nine of her life stories have been published in *Chicken Soup for the Soul* books including "The Power of Positive," "Touched by an Angel," and "Lemons to Lemonade." She also writes for *Christian Woman* magazine, *Kentucky Explorer, Lost Treasure*, plus many on-line websites and a column for her local paper.